For Allyn

Library of Congress Cataloging-in-Publication Data. Stock,
Catherine. Christmas time / by Catherine Stock. — 1st ed.
p.   cm. Summary: A child and her parents enjoy the last-
minute activities to prepare for Christmas.
ISBN 0-02-788403-1   [1. Christmas—Fiction.   2. Parent
and child—Fiction.]   I. Title.   PZ7.S8635Ch   1990
[E]—dc20   89-71249   CIP   AC

Christmas Time

BY CATHERINE STOCK

BRADBURY PRESS · NEW YORK

It's Christmas time. Outside, it's cold and snowy.

I put on my warm cap and mittens. We go to buy a Christmas tree.

"This one," I tell Daddy.

Mommy cuts up her old
magazines so that we can make
a long paper chain.

We wrap our chain around the tree. Then we hang shiny balls and tinsel on the branches. I help Daddy put a gold star right at the top.

At the store Daddy says,
"Don't you want to tell Santa
what you'd like for Christmas?"
There are too many people.
And there is too much noise.

Mommy says that we can write
to Santa instead.
"I want a fire truck," I say.
I stick the stamp on the
envelope and we mail the letter.

We bake Christmas cookies. I
make them pretty with raisins
and nuts and colored candy.

We sing carols with our friends.
I don't know all the words, but
when we sing "Jingle Bells," I
get to shake the sleigh bells.

It's Christmas Eve at last. Daddy
makes cocoa. We leave a mug for
Santa, too.

"Don't forget the carrots for
the reindeer," I say.

Then I hang up my stocking
at the end of my bed. I'll never
fall asleep!

But I do. Because suddenly it's morning and my stocking is full! Santa has left me a little teddy bear, a candy cane, and some chocolates.

And wrapped up under the
Christmas tree is a big red
fire truck!